Limbo

Part Two of
The Profane Comedy

D. Selby Fing
Illustrations by Bugs Pacino

NEW ACADEMIA PUBLISHING · SCARITH

Washington, DC

Library of Congress Control Number: 2024909675
ISBN 979-8-99005-42-33 (alk. paper)

 An imprint of New Academia Publishing

 New Academia Publishing
4401-A Connecticut Ave. NW, #236, Washington DC 20008
info@newacademia.com - www.newacademia.com

For my poetic guide
Grace Cavalieri

and my prosaic guide
Alice Stephens

Limbo

I knew I was being held as I fell,
As if the fire resisted my progress
I believed I was in the belly of hell

Being burned in order to manifest
The scars of one-third of understanding self –
If you have come thus far in a legitimate

Fashion – When implosion and the gravity
Of motion through atmospheres of fire
Brought me down to the ground, without levity,

Like an object drawn in to crashing by force,
Like a wave seeks the shore inevitably,
I came in with a howling shriek and a fierce

Impact which shattered my eggshell, but left me
Little traumatized. I was gasping for breath,
As if what had been taken from me, was bereft me,

Was like the finality of a single death,
Where the rest of the world kept itself progressing.
But it was clearly the beginning of a new path,

And as I stood up, the fire was above me,
Arrayed in the colors of dawn, and my guide
Returned beside me, offering a love he

Had not previously shown. He seemed relieved,
He smiled widely and he reached to hug me.
I appreciated that he seemed less aggrieved,

But I was still trying to make sense.
My mind was swollen with images, a river
Flowing with oceans of sentience

With no means to contain it all in structure
Like words, or language. My guide, with telling sapience,
Said: "It is not time for words yet, the scrivener   1263

Awaits." It was all new, but there was a pattern
Which I felt inclined to follow. We stood on a beach –
I hadn't noticed – at some distance, a lantern

Line 1263 - "It's not time for words yet, the scrivener awaits."

Burned at the historical site of Fort Phoenix,
At the north end of Buzzard's Bay. I felt concern
And familiarity for the light out of reach.

At the north of the harbor, New Bedford
Lay dimly against the crepuscular night sky
Before us, a man sat at a desk under the torch.

It was he, sparks flashing from the brow of his eye,
That we, like a hale father and wary son, approached
Without words, I knew again that it was not time

To reflect on what had come before or what
Was to come. My mind was soaked like a sponge,
With still yet more room to expand, but

Was it all just going to start again, the grunge
And vomit? I felt like asking if we could cut
To the important stuff and subsequently expunge,

From so much seeming detritus, the reason
For walking toward a man writing feverishly
At a desk on a beach at night, some ease from

The disconnected nature of these dreamishy
Revelations. I scuffed my feet on the sand and
The man looked up with eyes deliriously

Aggravated at our appearance. He flared his hands
And shouted, "How the hell did you get here?!"
He stood and marched directly at me with menace

Tightening that furious brow. He: "Hey there!"
Then he stopped. My Uncle stepped in front with feasance:
"Scribe, pay us the compliment of your grace, where

We are so obviously at your mercy." "I am no scribe,
Sir, but I shall be at your service if you are
Indeed who you seem to be. How shall I decide?"

I still could not speak, and did not recognize the man's glare,
But I nodded earnestly when his eyes met mine.
"Is he?" the scrivener sighed. "Only he could dare.

But tell me, sir, how have you come to land
Here at night, alone?" "It is dawn, sir, your lamp
Will soon be unnecessary." "But there it shall stand,

Until the sun prepares to pitch its camp
Tonight. None has ever appeared thus on strand.
I am befuddled. Who is this sorrowful tramp?   1305

Line 1305 - "Who is this sorrowful tramp?"

Did he wash up on the tide, having been cast adrift?
I have seen the look of men who have battled
The clenching jaws of death, suspended amidst

The briny, deflecting the sheer teeth of blood-addled
Sharks, with wooden planks for hours, then lifted
Into the hold of a buoyant boat, to regain balance,

To regain their lives, but not again in the same manner.
Such is the look of this newly hatched young man."
"An adept description. Now we must get to a tanner,

For he is rawhide which requires a tan.
He needs to stitch an emblem in his banner.
In this I mean to say that he will not be wan.

There is hope that he will be a good man someday.
He journeys hither to this noble end."
"It is no wonder then that you've come a different way."

I cleared my throat. "How do they normally come in?"
"You are a breather!" He stepped to touch me, "Hooray!
An interesting morning for me, my friend."

His beard and breath smelled like seaweed and grass.
His fingers were raw with some dermatitis
"I will answer your question and also will ask –

They arrive by boat an hour after sunrise.
How have you been granted this arduous task?"
"Lilica," I croaked in reply. I caught my guide's eyes.

He spoke eloquently: "Love is the purpose
Of our motion. This man refuses to relent
His allotted helix of time, although he curses

The very fate which created his helix.
We intend to rid him of the curses, of course
One cannot account for circumstances."

"I see," the sea-man scrivener said deeply.
He extended his hand to me. "Welcome
I am Melville. I will be good enough to set thee

On the proper path, for this appearance is so seldom.
But I must beg you not to linger too sweetly,
For I am a man with many stories and few words to tell them.

I write their names when they arrive in the boats
In the day time, and at night I write their stories.
I am given to ponder greatly upon their coats.

I see them so briefly. They arrive in flurries.
I remember the coats and envision their whole
Lives in the threads, their shabby or silken worries."

One flat-bottomed ferry boat emerged from the mist,
Just as the shadow of my body appeared
On the sand. Melville looked down and grinned at this.

He rubbed his cheeks, "By the soot in my beard!"
Mine was the only shadow. My fear increased,
Like I got on the wrong ride at the fair.

My Uncle touched my shoulder as the shadows disembarked:
"Do not let fear blind you to what you have done."
And Melville began repeating this single remark:

"I prefer not to." He went to his desk in the sun,
And sat and did nothing until it was dark,
As far as I could tell. I asked my guide, "Does this one

Guard the gate?" "In his manner he is definitive."
"But the same could be said for all of us."
"As the guards change at the gate of Perdition,

So they change here. There is no guarantor for us:
You either make it here on your journey, deliberately,
Or not. The gate is just what you walk through."

We walked with the last of the shadows and my guide,
Not presuming the others were on the proper path,
Asked Melville: "Should we follow the crowd, scribe?"

"I prefer not to." "No, you mean…" and we all laughed.
Even Melville, who widely grinned and sighed,
"Yes, just follow the crowd into sackcloth and ash,

Although, I prefer not to." In the dusky gloam
Of a temperate morning, we walked with the shadows.
I: "I know this town. My fathers called it their home."

My guide: "I doubt you know it now, but who knows?
No two occurrences happen in exactly the same poem
In the same manner, ever. We shall see what comes and goes."

"But if I recognize the town, it is consistent,
In some regard with some time before."
"Still, is not the city like a body, persistent

Despite its slow and steady, if not boring,
Metamorphic and striving development,
Its self-overcoming and gestational restoring.

Change in infinite repetition and endless
Variation. Do not think that because it is alike
Then it is the same. But of course, you know this."

"I think so, sir. The same, but different, like
Twins, or clones. It makes me doubtful of the essence
Of my reasoning in my panic-stricken life."

"As well it should, because you are about to atone
For that self-same dubious essence of reasoning."
"What?" "This is your journey. The forsaken are alone,

But you are joining with others who are lessening
The weights they have to carry as they seek Tlön,
Those who are moving toward releasing

Themselves from themselves as a disciplined attainment."
"You've been here before?" "My son, this is where I reside.
I am here for an eternity of atonement."

"But who is Tlön, and how does he decide?"
"Tlön is what is to come, gravity, light, the attunement
Of all waves of energy into the spiral, beside

Which, there is nothing." "So we are moving toward it?"
"As it moves toward us, and goes beyond us.
Lilica will show you how to regard it

From a better perspective, without the despondence
Of these weights." "What weights?" At this moment a disabled
Boy with squinting eyes, drool, and jutted double chins

Approached us, speaking mutely, as if the sound
Were swirling about in his empty head before
Coming out as: "Gummawn. Gummawn. Gummawn."

He brought us to the docks, and the boats were ashore.   1411
Men were unloading a cornucopia of tons
Of Atlantic cod, salmon, lobster and swordfish.

Line 1411 - He brought us to the docks and the boats were ashore.

The boy/man took up his task with a knife
And gutted every fish he could get a grip on.
He sang drunkenly the only song in his life:

"Michael rowed the boat ashore, alleluia," flipping
The bloody innards wherever they flew off,
And grabbing the next writhing body for ripping.

He said: "My name is Jack." And then an incongruous
Man in a tuxedo appeared. He carried a tuna,
Which could not possibly have been more enormous,

And wore the man's stove-pipe hat, singing, "Oh, moon, ahh,
You are lovely this evening. I am Millard Fillmore."
"And yet, you are a fish," replied my Uncle.

"We," the tuna continued, "are souls conjoined.
But soon we will be taking the next step."
"What is the next step?" I asked in a voice resigned

To incomprehension, as if all language were a trap.
"I don't know, but it is not down. We have been consigned
To the dustbin, but at least we have our strap,"

The silent man raised his left hand to reveal
A leather strap of six-inch length, "So we stay
Together and connect to Tlön when the wheel

Turns in our favor." "Will you tell us, pray,"
My guide requested, "For what sin you've been brought to heel?"
"The same as you, my friend, but different in the way

I manifested it – by supporting an unjust law.
I could not unite the divided ideal,
And I sided with compromise – that's the flaw –

Where compromise was just a corrupt deal.
This so offended my constituency, and Tlön,
That we never wore Whigs again, and I am here,

Carrying weights over distances of time
Which the living cannot conceive." The smell
Was of salt flesh. Jack scrambled gaily to climb

The mountain of fish drowning on air at sea level.
He came down with a sac of guts, which he cut with his knife
And a million black eggs poured out on the gravel.

The pile began writhing and twisting up to form
Another human being. A squat man like Jack,
With a wide round belly, but clearer-voiced and normal

Around the eyes. The man shivered up his back
And became animated when the eggs stopped pouring.
What had only been a gelatinous mass

Was transformed into a Master Debater:
"Stephen Douglas, at your service, if you so wish…
I see you are again with us, Honest Abe."

"And where I am, you are not far behind, with fish
Eggs to perpetuate your philosophy of hatred."
"The people will always find a way to express

Their will." "There is always someone to pander
To them, I concur, but that doesn't make them right or true."
"This government requires an interpreter

Of the babel of voices from below.
Just because I am, for the enfranchised, representor
Does not mean that I am without value."

My Uncle smiled without relent: "Lives play out.
History judges. Some who call themselves heroes
Shrink into oblivion. Small men who sow doubt,

No matter their millions, end up with zeroes."
Douglas: "Which is all one needs to enter from without."
Lincoln assented: "Equality begins at zero.

It is responsibility which adds quantity,
In an accumulation of actions to the good
And sincerity of pursuit which adds quality

To the purpose of existence. Our falsehood,
Our failure to live up to such ideals, to verify
The positive in our lives, is the reason why

We are sent here." Jack still stood grinning,
Holding Douglas' head. I: "Why is he here?"
"He just is," my guide said. "You might find he is spinning

Wisdom. Have you any questions for our dear
Adversary?" "Aren't you sorry for continuing   1484
To sustain the moral fissure in our country?"

Line 1484 - "Aren't you sorry for sustaining the moral fissure in our country?"

"My good man, I am a sac of fish eggs
What need or use have I for sorrow?
People can't just leave a question when it begs,

They have to find out what you will say tomorrow.
Well, I have no insights, as I have no legs.
Anything I could give you I would have to borrow."

I to my guide: "He is on the path to redemption?"
"Tlön is not redemption, but there is more to see."
Just then we were passed by hundreds of fishermen

Who were clearly off the clock and free
To wander the dock in search of refreshment.
Jack let go of Douglas' head and he,

As any Little Giant would, crumpled to the ground
Amidst the tonnage of bloody innards scattered,
Like all that is useless and yet occupies space, around

Our feet. Jack said, "Gummawn," and trundled with the sea-battered 1501
Men, cracked skin and hoary beards, as they found
The first shanty bar they could find. We gathered

With them at the door, but we were slow getting in,
Because everyone had to put on a hair-shirt.
"Me too?" I asked warily, watching the grim men

Settle in with their illusions dashed, but still thirsty.
"Yes," my guide said heavily. I felt like telling him,
Once again, that I was unready for another first,

Never having worn a hair-shirt before.
My Uncle scowled at my hesitation:
"Don't you see that this will someday be over?

Line 1501 - Jack said, "Gummawn," and trundled with the sea'-battered/Men.

Don't you want to feel as much sensation
As you can garner on this journey? Knowledge is power.
Or must you wait for Lilica to see revelation?"

I sighed, put on the barbed cloth, and entered
The quietest bar I'd ever seen. No music,
No billiards, no waitress, no bartender.

There was a monkey at an open window, using
A bucket to scoop scummy salt water from under
The dock. Some of the men drank this fluid

Out of angry desperation, but they were not sated.
And they grumbled as they scratched at their rawing chests.
My skin felt the same; the hair shirt agitated

A fiery irritation, worsened by sweat.
I heard a man shout, "This place was created   1526
For whiskey. But there's no whiskey for the guests!

I would gladly pay you Tuesday, for a whiskey today."
My guide harkened: "I know that tobacco voice."
Jack snuffled and shuffled off toward the braying.

Line 1526 - "This place was created/For whiskey."

His eyes seemed closed all the time, like chance
Was his only option. But he laughed as he swayed
Into the crowd of aggravated seamen, like an advance

Guard. As an anomaly, he was not well met
By the tobacco-voiced man and those surrounding
Him. They gazed into the space they left

As they backed away and gawked at the astounding
Vision of moon-faced Jack. They seemed miffed
That he had no bottle. They started pounding

The tables and stamping the floor: "Whiskey! Whiskey!"
Jack laughed and slapped his thighs. I followed my guide,
Though he was slowed by the crowd. Then he beckoned: "Ulysses."

The crowd went silent. I wanted to hide,
For they were menacing and dry. But their leader was
General Grant, appearing more general than martial. I'd

Have spoken but only Jack could be heard breathing
When their eyes locked onto each other. Not lovers,
For that would be too strong, but they were seething

With knowledge of and love for the other.
My Uncle said: "It's always good to have this meeting."
Grant replied: "I forget that you are coming."

They embraced beside Jack, who hugged them as well;
My guide so tall, Grant so ragged, and Jack so wide.
Only Jack had no tears to wipe away from the swell

Of emotion that coursed through that room – a tide
Undeniable. And Lincoln said: "We have come from hell,   1556
And we have bourbon!" Jack then produced a vial,

The thickness of his thumb, which he gave to Grant.
He uncorked it and took a tentative draft.
"Aaahhh," he sighed and inhaled, "This helps make one endurant.

This shirt is flaying me!" He drank again and laughed:
"Do you know when this campaign ends, Mr. President?"
"Mine ends before yours. Beyond Tlön, none of this lasts.

Yet great things lay in store, for those who can envision
And always progress, like a slow-moving arrow
At an ever-present target, in that direction."

Line 1556 - "We have come from hell,/And we have bourbon."

Grant drank again. He saw his men, their narrow
Minds upon the vial in his hand. They would sanction
Murder to get a swig of that barley juice, fair, oh!

"May I, Mr. President, share this with my men?"
"It is only fitting." He turned his palm to Jack,
Who giggled and brought forth a dozen vials twice again

From the pockets of his trousers. His teeth were black
And shiny when he smiled in the gray light, a friend
To each sea-ravaged salt. And they gulped it back.

And they could not drain the tiny vials.
I was only allowed to continue to wear
The hair-shirt. I did not ask for a swallow

For fear of some dreadful consequence. I dared
Not bend toward the temporal valleys
If I still had deserts to go before there –

Wherever there was – It was a space filled
With light. The seamen began singing shanty songs,
Taking enormous draughts from the thin pill

Bottles, and I watched as my guide resisted their throng,
Who wanted to loft him up in a chair and call him
Messiah, which my guide would have none of, longing

Only to witness their pleasure from a certain distance.
Jack wanted a ride in the chair, and so
The hungry men, drunk instantaneously,

Hoisted him upon their shoulders and to and fro
Danced about the joyful bar, Jack the ring master.
This made my guide smile. He touched Grant's shoulder though

It was a wistful touch. And Grant said: "Thank you
We will remain hungover until your return."
"Yes," my Uncle seemed more fatigued in the dank brew

Hall, "We are all condemned to eternal relearning."
"But," Grant said earnestly, "It is better since you
Have passed through. Now we shall suffer our burning

Less. Our souls shall be freed of the habits
Which institutions make it their purpose
To encase us within." My guide only said, "Perhaps."

"I want to believe it is so." "Then I provide a service."
"More than that, you are the reason for the vast
Implication of this union upon world history.

I just rode your coattails." My guide smiled again:
"Better you than McClellan." The men set down Jack.
It was clear that we would be off, but then

Jack had some difficulty getting the bottles back.
The men were reluctant, but with a gesture from Grant,
They relinquished the joyful vials which they lacked

Every other moment of their eternal lives,
At which point the hair-shirt melted off my chest.
The cool air against my swollen and sweaty hives

Was enough to make me drunk, and we rejoiced.
We were no longer stuck in this shanty dive.
Grant spoke: "Let us be after new engagements,

And fare thee well, Mr. President, your honor."
The tears in Grant's eyes kept my Uncle from chastising
Him his formality, but he said, "We are on our

Journey together, even if we are practicing
Our punishments apart." "I'd be a goner…"
Grant wiped his nose on his sleeve and ceased soliloquizing.

No further words were spoken and Jack lead us out.
My guide had no doubt about where to go next.
"Where do they go next?" I asked. He: "I believe they have the gout

Next, but there will be cushions and iced cakes.
So it's a step up, though they have forgotten about
Me already. I'm not as important as he thinks."

Jack sang: "Michael rowed the boat ashore, alleluia."
I looked up Union Street, up the hillside.   1631
I saw the quintessential America,

Line 1631 - I looked up Union Street, up the hillside./I saw the quintessential America.

Commerce first and a fairly steep incline
Up, past the churches, into the neighborhoods,
Where people began over and over again

A new life in a new world of potential.
Seeking to find the means to spark kinesis –
Civility, liberty, faith in the providential –

They worked to claim for themselves successes
In the material world, despite the decadential
Nature of that accumulating synthesis.

"But first," my Uncle interrupted my day dream,
Turning into the shop under the sign 'Old Hickory's',   1643
We must get thee to the tannery."

"Must get me?" I retorted for it had a prickery
Sound. "What exactly is our tanning need?"
And my Captain: "He who would attain victory

Must endure the torment of the vanquished.
Rawhide has fewer uses than leather."
My face must have worn my body's anguish.

My guide: "How can you fear the weight of a feather
In the face of an eternity of relinquishment?"
"I don't know what you are asking me to weather."

Andrew Jackson stepped out of the shadows,
Long-jawed and wild, the gilded brass knuckles
Of the Enlightenment, storming from the south.

He was accoutered as a Roman, with buckles
Holding fast his maroon tunic. His cold mouth
Was black when it opened and he spoke: "Fuckles,

Line 1643 - Turning into the shop under the sign 'Old Hickory's'

I'm gonna tan your hide, man!" I: "What is
Fuckles? What is that?" He: "That is my name for you,
You turd. You are Fuckles. So strip and give us a kiss."

I looked to my Uncle and asked, "Is it true?"
Jack was taking off his pants. "Not you moron!"
Jackson roared, and turned to me, "This is yours to do

Your Captain can only take you so far
And then you are on your own. I have waited
For a breather to come through. I'm for war

And receiving my due. And both were made
To experience and pursue. How can power
Otherwise prove? How can you bestride

The hobby-horse of your vocation without
A little wear in the seat?" Said I: "No."
Jackson looked to my guide without any doubt.

"Do not be afraid of what you don't know.
Your body was made to receive and to push out.
Physicality is what leads to gnosis.

It's time for me to go now." I had dread;
Jackson bent me over a pine counter, tying
My ankles to hooks at the floor, spread

Wider than my shoulders. My wrists were together,
Arms stretched across the counter, hooked to
Something on the other side by a leather

Strap. I was prone and trembling: "Oh my god."
And he: "There is no god and this is your life whether
You enjoy it or not." He took out and shook

A cat-o'nine-tails, saying, "Would you cease
To exist for this rape, or will you become
Of greater use to humanity?"

I: "You speak of humanity to a man
Whose asshole you are about to penetrate
With your syphilitic, pus-caked penis."

"So what more needs to be said?" and he commenced
The deed, first by whipping my thighs and buttocks.
I shook cold sweat and the welts were intense.

Jackson mumbled and fumbled with his own bollocks.
He dropped the whip, lifting the tunic with his immense
Erection. I thought: "This is going to happen. Mollusk."

And Lilica appeared before me, her face   1699
And body swaying with the wooden columns
Beyond the counter where I was placed.

Line 1699 - And Lilica appeared before me.

She was not radiant but gray and solemn:
"Oh my brother. It is not easy to be chaste.
The only purity expected in Tlön

Is that which you have conjured, like an oyster
Takes a grain of sand to create a pearl.
We love you and wish to wipe the moisture

From your eyes. Do not fail to see the world
Of love which awaits you, beyond this cloister   1708
Of misery, repentance, and peril."

Jackson grunted and shuddered and tucking
His flaccifying penis under his tunic, spoke:
"And expect it to get worse, for fucking

Line 1708 - "Do not fail to see the world/Of love which awaits you..."

Will come under any manner of cloak,
In the form of a gun or the sucking
Of the value of your life into a joke."

I presumed, with semen dribbling down
My leg, that I was at the bottom, done.
I could not see up and my anus unwound,

As if I had taken an enormous shit
And it had forced its way back into me,
Whereupon I pushed it out again, etc…

Lilica did not inspire me so much
As she reminded me how far I seemed
From contentment with my own condition.

And who would be content? And where were Jack
And my guide? Why this abandonment? Tears fell   1727
Out of my eyes onto the dry wooden floor

Of the tannery. I was untied and I stood
Looking up at the support beams of the roof.
The future would be both worse and better,

The same, but different. I pulled up my pants
And left without a word to the smirking
Tanner and his manifest destiny. I glanced

Down Union Street and saw the city working,
Industrious and spiritless, they advanced,
With the purpose of never ever shirking

In their accumulation of wealth to evidence
Their state of grace in the material realm;
They alone, like me, but aware of the precedence

Line 1727 - Why this abandonment?

Of nothing over themselves. I suspected this balm,
For all understanding is self-deceptence;
If one propels one's self forward with calm

Acceptance of the futility of endeavor,
There can only be assurance that vanity
Is the virtue of this age, and that anyone

Can be vain about their insanity,
Their failures, weaknesses and quivering
Resolutions. These are not calamities,

They are the foundation of a moral system,
Based on the supremacy of the self,
Which supplies all with equality of rights,

If not equality of opportunity.
I was saddle-sore, and I was remembering
Only Lilica, how she was careless, but there.

She could have been anywhere else, and was,
But she was also with me, in me
So that I could know that there is something

Other than me, when I'm taking it in the ass.
Lilica was only a shade different
From the black heart rapist tanner, another

Napoleon, King of New Orleans, Backwater
Sutpen writ in granite conquest of the continent,
Genocide, segregation, exploitation

Of the lowest classes, the minorities
Who become the scapegoats of the flaws
Of the poor white people who ritualistically

Oppress them by means of institutions
Of the majority, by the majority,
For the majority corrupted by racism,

Ignorant of their denial, and he
Is their leader, who would rape them
Because they breathe, but she was not the same.

She was there to ease the visceral shock
And that she did. What more need I? Alone
On Union Street in cobblestone New Bedford

A place which my fathers had yet to arrive,
But they were feeling the beginnings of famine,
Which would force them to find and start at the bottom

Rung of the bottomless ladder of America,
The only thing I must do is get through this obsession
And acknowledge that others have sweated too

To alter the form of my sweating, for better
Or worse. And I must love Lilica, and Lincoln,
And Jack, for the fact that they give me anything

At all. The rest is mine to regard as I please
Knowing though that when I think of her projecting
Her negativity onto me, I also do the reverse.

As I took my first step uphill, alone,
My Captain returned with good fellow Jack,
Who wore the face of Jesus' pity

As he gazed into my eyes on the street.
My uncle: "I go to the theater tonight."
"Here, in town?" I replied, wondering whether

We were going to speak of my rape,
But I would not instigate a tawdry
Recounting of what I had no recollection

Thanks, I suppose, to Lilica who took
The experience away from me, although
My body told me, as I walked, that it

Had happened. My guide wanted to see a show.
Under any other circumstance, it would seem
Normal. "Uncle, is there an end in sight?"

Jack began singing, "Michael rowed the boat ashore,
Alleluia." "One can always imagine an end,"
My uncle said, "And one can always make

An end out of any old thing, but they
Are always bound up with beginnings,
Which must be acknowledged for balance.

Time keeps moving, ends recur." I sensed
His gravity and said, "You have been here before."
"And I cannot go with you to meet Lilica."

"Where are we going?!" "It's Ford's Theater, right here,   1813
On Union Street." We turned into a gas-lit lobby,
Dressed in evening clothes, and the crowd were not

Unanimous in their high regard for my guide.
I noted hostility in the eyes above the beards
In the milling crowd. Jack shuffled behind me,

Line 1813 - "It's Ford's Theater, right here,/On Union Street."

Groaning rhythmically, wary, anxious, scared.
He held my hand as a path opened up for us
To ascend the stairs to the balcony.

My Captain remained composed, unsmiling,
And aloof from the buzz he generated,
His head disappeared first into the darkness

Into a scene I well knew. Jack began weeping
Openly, but it was as if no other person
Could see him sob or the tears sweeping

Down his syndromic cheeks. I called out, "Please."
Cringing in mad terror, yet we kept moving
Up each step inexorably, I repeat,

Against my will we joined our guide in the booth.   1831
It was an aleph moment for me:
I saw all that has been and is to be, and both

Line 1831 - Against my will we joined our Guide in the booth.

Had me twitching in impending panic.
I saw Jesus and Nietzsche together,
Resting as would a lion with a lamb.

I saw how every stone in the earth was formed and
encrusted, stratified and impacted, I saw the desert and
the ocean switching sides, I saw all the mothers and all
the fathers in an angry primal scene, I saw the capillaries
dilating of all the eyes made sore by the dust of the wind-
swept land, I saw five billion suns set and rise for ten billion
years on twenty trillion planets, I saw every wave that ever
washed on every shore…

I sat petrified now, like a sculpture
In a bad place. And he to me: "I told thee I
Would have to leave. Do not be unstable

As you grieve. Promise me you will also sing
The song of the bleeding throat,
Death's outlet song of life, (for well dear brother I know,
If thou wast not granted to sing thou would'st surely die.)
Rest, ye now, you have yet more traveling in the morning."

I tried to say, "I cannot leave you behind
I cannot let you die." But I could not move.
The show commenced. Jack wailed, his face in his hands.

I was breathing steadily, but I cannot prove
It. And then I saw the gun, and the shade glanced
At me as he took the last steps on his hooves.

The gun did not waver and the shots rang out.
Lincoln fell forward and off his chair.
The man named Booth leapt over the railing,

Shouting, "Sic semper tyrannis." Out of the air
He fell and broke his leg, "Oh!" he sang out.
Jack and I were not freed and held fast where

We were, crying now in pity and fear,
While the crowd gathered and took him away.
I cried until my body ached and tears

Ran like salt canyons down my face,
Until, when we were finally released,
We collapsed in a pile in that place.

I woke to Jack singing, "Michael rowed the boat
Ashore, alleluia." He was out of key,
And solemn, but also contented. He spoke:

"Uncle is gone. Gummawn. Gummawn. With me."
I felt refreshed with the first sleep I had broke
In I couldn't remember. It seemed a mystery,

Like I had been on this journey all my life,
With someone to lead me and now I needed to
Go on on my own. Such is the nature of strife

That its rewards are equally indebted to
The proportion of suffering, if the sacrifice
Is sincere in the name of its resolution.

I stood with Jack and we left the theater.
Bells sounded down the hillside and the coffin
Was being drawn down Union Street, crowds gathered

In silence to grieve as they don't get to often
To recognize a person who knew what mattered,
And whose words would redound across time

And would give opportunity free reign,
For some, and eventually, perhaps never, all.
Jack produced a flowering branch and gave

It to me. I walked over and let it fall
Upon the cart which drew the black cage
Saying, "Here coffin that slowly passes,   1893
I give you my sprig of lilac."

And he went forward hence with the disabled man,
Not a follower, but not leading, where they would go,
Up Union Street, while the tearful crowd ignored them,

Going down to pay their respects. Who could know
How to carry on without their guide? "Gummawn."
He: "He is still with us." Jack smiled: "I know."

Line 1893 - "'Here coffin that slowly passes,/I give you my sprig of lilac.'"

At the moment when he began to wonder
In earnest over what would come next, a shadow
Fell upon the two, in the shape of a thunderous

Top hat, stealing from an alley, grabbing at his elbow.
More gloam than substance, it hissed: "They blunder
Who will destroy Reconstruction to gain power."

"Are you real?" said Fing. "I smell you more than I see."
"Indeed, I am the smoke of the candle gone out   1908
A dissipation, a wisping trace of history."

"Please tell me the purpose of your picking me out."
"I am the past returning differently,
But the same, as a warning to the complacent,

Line 1908 - "I am the smoke of the candle gone out..."

They alter the structure of the nation
Who manipulate the levers of state,
By means of the influence of corporation,

And media. They will sell freedom to the greatest
Bidder. And it will require generations
To overcome what will be lost in the glitter."

"What is the source of your prophetic claim?"
"Experience," whispered the mist. "I am Tilden."
The Wayfarer did not recognize the name,

"I'm sorry, have I heard of your children?"
"History is supposed to proclaim
Its winners, and yet I have become its victim.

I won an election but lost the Presidency,
At the hands of the power brokers behind
The scenes, and their pitiless expediency

Laid the foundation for the continuing bind
Of racial relations and the tendency
For all to lay more claim to their civil rights,

Thereby fracturing the country by their deferral,
Which truly is the same old story around here.
Even the war couldn't alter our feral

Truth." Then Fing smelled the body of the crowd near
By, and the vaporous Tilden was gone. The veil
Was lifted. One man more joined then in careering

Against the flow of mourners, up Union Street,
Toward the neighborhoods of widow's walks,
Where children can find their mother's tears incomplete.

Line 1941 - ...he was Frederick Douglass, deep and fleet,
          Elbow out in front.

Fing knew by the cut of the neck of the man's cloak,
That he was Frederick Douglass, deep and fleet,   1941
Elbow out in front. Fing: "Sir, do you have hope

Also, that this is the proper direction?"
"I know it is, yes." His chin jutted as the prow
Of a ship in high seas. Their progression

Eased. "You know us not," Fing said, "yet you plow
Through the crowd in our assistance." "A mission,
You might call it." "So, you knew to be here now?"

Jack chuckled and began humming again,
As if the burden of grieving had ceased.
Fing pondered: "You know why I am here, then?"

"In part," Douglass began, "You did not believe
In yourself, but you have been chosen among men
To invert the understanding of peace

By dreaming and waking and writing down words."
"Peace?! How can anybody believe in that?
And how can words convey something so absurd?"

Douglass gave no answer, leaving Fing in a vat
Of blubbery confusion: "All I've seen is turds!
I just got butt-fucked by Andrew Jackson!"

"Welcome to the club," said the self-freed slave,
"We have received the same for four hundred years.
My people are marginalized in their graves.

You didn't see any blacks in your ring of tears."
Fing was ashamed, "No, but am I to blame?"
Douglass was again silent. Fing: "My fear is

That I won't know how to represent you."
"That is a start," Douglass smiled, "It's not your job."
They continued up Union Street.

Gertrude Stein arrived then saying, "Endless repetition
Infinite Variation, endless repetition infinite variation
Endless repetition, infinite variation."

Fing astounded as she took her place next to Douglass,
Thrusting her elbow forward, shouting, "Back, back,"
Winnowing a way out of the thronging mass,

Who wept down the hillside toward the vacuum,
Where gravity has left the whole of greatness
Into nothing, which fades as lightning crack.

Fing wept too: "That man hath given me glass
For my eyes, absurd but not spectacular.
I have seen scarlet waves billowing past,

And lead by presentations oracular,
To this summit in New England, long since past
Reason. Are either of you prognosticators?"

Jack sang, "Michael rowed the boat ashore, alleluia."
Gertrude Stein looked anxiously at his singing.
Fing shouted: "Him?!" Jack, where are we going?" "Lilica,

Can't you smell her?" Gertrude Stein was snarling,
"I can smell her. Oh, yes." She inhaled deeply.
"She is Columbia, the eagle's eye, the starling,

Valiant and inclusive. She is love, you can smell her."
Fing: "Jack, how much further? Where is she?"
"We turn north on County." "Is that all? Can you tell her

We are coming?" "She knows," hissed Douglass, "It's we
Who do not know. But I do smell her. Nothing sweeter."
"She is love for all," said Jack, "Opportunity."

"I just smell fish," sighed Fing. "That's her," drooled Stein,
"A man cannot know such love from the earth.
The fecund, salty abundance of the ocean.

The clouds and the rain, the loam and the delta.
There is too much manufacture in a man's devotion.   2001
Why, you think of the world in terms of its dearth!

How did you have the gall to claim it for your own,
To feel entitled to perpetuating the claim,
To paving it over so that no one could say, 'No!'?"

Line 2001 - "There is too much manufacture in a man's devotion."

"Do I have to accept more of the blame,"
Asked Fing, in righteous self-defense, "To go on
And see Lilica?" Douglass laughed: "No, just play the game.

We are almost there." Gertrude Stein spoke no more,
Aiding them in turning on County Street.
Then she pointed to the St. Lawrence Church door.

Jack: "We must be purified in the sacristy."
Fing walked about the dim church on the squeaky floor
"This is the church my grandmother used to be

Involved in." Douglass pointed above the altar:
"Is that her?" "Good fucking Jesus!" Fing shouted.
"They've crucified my grandmother!"

There she hung, white linens tastefully draped
Over her wizened, brittle, corpulent torso,
Nails driven through her hands. Her fingers

Were arthritically curled over her palms.
Jack: "We must purify the sacristy now."
Fing: "I hope you mean that we should give alms.

How can I get my grandmother down?"
Douglass whispered urgently, "Forget your problems.
She is where she wanted to be found.

You need to be dry to continue this quest."
Fing: "I haven't had a drink since Grant."
Then the barber entered, "At your request."

"Not my request," Fing objected, but cant
Failed him in this case as well. Douglass pressed
Him against the first pew, holding him at ankles

And wrists. Then the barber brought out the leeches,   2033
Attaching them to Fing's arms and chest. He retched,
From the smell of forensic brine, beseeching:

"They don't do this anymore! And why in church?!"
The barber cut the bottoms of the hirudo medicinalis,
"For faster service." Jack nodded: "Keep courage."

Line # 2033 - The barber brought out the leeches,
            Attaching them to Fing's arms and chest.

"You aren't being purified!" "But I am leading us."
"By the smell of fish in the harbor? And this is the charge
For your service?" Jack scowled: "This discipline is

Your reward, your path to freedom. There is no
Other option. Consciousness is a cage.
The body is not made to sustain consciousness.

There is nothing else besides this tragic stage
And that is what makes it so humorous.
Did you know that Michael was an avenging angel?"

Fing let his blood flow out. It didn't belong to him.
The blood poured out of the leeches onto the floor.
They all went pale. Fing ceased to feel the dim

Darkness of the church, the weight of his corpse.
Transformed and dry, he rose and limned
His lack of feeling thus: "I have been through a small door

And now I am expanding in the space
On the other side." Douglass took Fing's hand
To keep him from floating off and Jack gazed

Out, sniffing. "Gummawn. Gummawn." "Leave the damned
Behind," Douglass exhorted. "Embrace the next phase."
Dessicated, but buoyant, Fing asked, "This is planned,

Right?" His feet and shoulders hovered parallel
To the ground. Douglass tugged at Fing's arm,
Down the aisle and out of the cathedral,

Like a child pulls a balloon, string in palm.
They began to ascend a decahedral
Tower, by cramped wooden stairs, a balm

To Fing's anxiety about floating away.
Still he could not get his feet to the floor
And bumped along at Douglass' sway,

Up and to the right. Fing: "Can you tell me more,
Douglass?" "Some of us will be walking this way
Down." Baffled, Fing then heard a man moaning, "Lenore!"

He saw a body fall past a small window,
And the moaning man descending the stairs.
The man saw the body falling too and cried, "Oh!"

And continued blubbering his wails.
Fing: "Douglass, this man is Edgar Allan Poe.
Will you please ask him why he fares so?"

Poe: "I heard the words this young breather hath spoken,
And I know in my chamber what hauntings cobwebs hold,
So I must take my eyes out to forestall choking

On my tears." Fing: "Is what I ask too bold?"
"No, sir," quoth Poe, "I have a third one, hopefully."
He tucked his eyes into this vest pockets, then tolled:

"For whom shall I cry anyway?" Fing: "Did you bring
The person who just fell up to the top?"
"She didn't fall up! Ahhhhh!" Poe began crying

Again: "Neither will you." Fing: "So I am to drop."
"She's gone to heaven," Poe sobbed, "I am dying!"
Fing: "But I am lighter than air, what is to stop

Me from drifting into the clouds? Am I not
Falling up right now?" Douglass mentioned:
"The higher you go, the further you fall. Got it?"

"That is why I am so guilty," Poe said, wrenching
Over in spasms. He produced from his vest pocket
A long thin needle. "No lovers have loved so intensely

As we. I had to ensure that she fell down.
Our love was seraphic, which the angels envied.
I was not wicked to give her to Tlön.   2098

I was not wicked to give her to Tlön.
I was not wicked to give her to Tlön."
Poe hurried down the stairs now at great speed

Line 2098 - "I was not wicked to give her to Tlon."

Stabbing at the eyes in his vest pocket
With the long thin needle, crying, "Lenore!"
Fing felt more reluctant to continue, but mocked

Poe, "Love will do that to me no more.
But is he a guide like you? He seemed so shocked
At the bizarrity of his own behavior."

Douglass replied: "He will remain in Limbo,
A guide to those who, like yourself, waver."
Fing: "How can he guide anybody? He is so

Blind." "A man need not only sweetness to savor
His sensation of taste." "Has he some sin, though,
Which enthralls him in this surreal haven?

How is it that you cannot reach heaven?
And how can I if I float into the sky?"
Douglass, pulling Fing's arm, commenced ascension:

"Nobody knows, or can tell you, the reason why.
Start at ten and go halfway and halfway again;
Halfway will never reach eleven, even if you try."

Fing: "So how will I attain this transition?"
Douglass: "In time." At which moment a chaos
Arose from below, not outside but within,

From behind, where Poe had recently passed.
Douglass: "It's Texas, I'll bet, making that din.
They always howl about their due payoff."

A cluttering wagon train of pioneers
Rumbled up the stairway. Fing heard cries, "Hey!
Let us in! We're coming in! We're bringing steers!"

The well-dressed leader, with aquiline nose, said: "Wait."
And the wagon train, far too vast to climb the thin stairs,
Slowed to a dusty halt. "I am Tyler. I bring this state   2131

Line 2131 - "I am Tyler. I bring this state
          To the paradise of the future, to the Union."

To the paradise of the future, to the Union."
The rabble behind him crowed, "We bring ourselves!
We demand entry! We've got numbers and guns!"

Tyler raised his palm: "Remember the Alamos
Of your past." The crowd ceased to shout their opinions,
Lowering their heads as in reverence.

"Let us through," Tyler hissed, "Or prepare for battle.
We will have democracy, one way or another."
Douglass smiled: "Easy now. How will these cattle

Pass us on these narrow steps?" "They have come thus far
Through impossibility. It is not hard to trample
An enemy. Triumph is all that matters."

"I am not your enemy. I am a citizen."
"You are a black man, an escaped slave."
Fing: "I am white. To me, will you listen?"

"You are a white man with a child and a slave.
History insists we shall pass and enter in.
Do you dare deny us what we crave?

We are the majority. We will persist."
Douglass: "You are carpetbaggers and scamps!
You believe in some right, which does not exist,

To exploit the land and burn electric lamps,
But your energy will soon enough desist.
You will choke on your numbers and your dams."   2155

Tyler smiled snidely: "And still we shall pass."
Douglass: "Not all who pass arrive at their destination."
"How can we fail, being the ruling mass?

But I'll not quibble with a man of your station.
Only let us through, we have history to catch,"
Spoke the lean man, the rest nodding assignation.

"You shall be caught indeed," Douglass responded,
"If you could forestall your rush, you might see,
But apparently your reason has absconded

Due to the pressure of your avarice and greed."
Douglass relented and the three stood aside.
The passers-by, the Texans, spat upon the three,

Line 2155 - "You will choke on your numbers and your dams."

Although more wrathfully upon Douglass and Jack,
As they ascended the spiralling tower stairs.
Fing was irate: "How can this be happening?"

Douglass remained composed, despite the trampling steer:
"Justice exists in every crevice of fact.
Do not wonder at those who appear   2173

To be surpassing, for they can be lost in air;
And those who fall to the ground are held dear,
Despite what outward progress may declare.

Tlön makes such differentiation clear
By the institutions of its disciplinary
Regimes. The manifestations of its structure.

Line 2173 - "Do not wonder at those who appear
            To be surpassing, for they can be lost in air..."

All else is dissipated into ether,
But of that we have not any fear,
Unless it were made into a scripture;

That is why you have been through perdition,
And limbo, to know better what is of no use
And what is. Ideology's ambition

Is to ignore its ridiculous failures,
And to always believe in what it may win
For its own glory or some such excuse.

You may help to remind them, in your way."
Fing, befuddled: "You mean they will not see
Tlön?" "Like lemmings they will leap," Spoke the gray

Line 2198 - "...they think they have light," he slowed and sighed,
            "When all they have is electricity
            And its manifestations."

Man, "Yet they will not fall. Instead they will be
Dispersed by eddying breezes to dissipate,
To become of no consequence, as darkness seems

When light penetrates. They will become dreams."
"Why don't they just stop leaping?" Fing replied.
"They believe in what they are doing. They are free,

But they think they have light," he slowed and sighed,   2198
"When all they have is electricity
And its manifestations." Jack again climbed

The steps, with Douglass and Fing following.
Fing: "No small thing, electric light, don't you think?"
"Materially, for some. But come the harrowing,

They shall be swept like water down a sink.
No control over their environment,
Just submission to its dictatorial stink,"

Douglass stopped and looked at Fing, "You know
That I will not go with you. I will stay."
Fing considered: "How will I fall into Tlön?

Tell me, how will I not just float away?
Do you have long thin needle, like Poe?"
Douglass nodded at the lumbering sway

Of Jack, the lowly king, who turned and grunted,
"Gummawn. Gummawn. Gummawn. Gummawn. Gummawn."   2214
Fing, weightless, could not understand: "How is this stunted,

Shuffling boy-man going to deliver me to Tlön?"
"You must hold on to him when he is shunted,
For, after this journey, he will go down."

Fing somewhat deflated: "But I would not."
Douglass: "But you will, with Jack. And Lilica
Will meet you on the other side. You will know what

Beauty is. You won't want to go back."
"You say I will be going back, but
I don't remember what I left. What of Jack?"

"He meets Tlön on impact, and goes on without you."
"He is like a savior." "Call him what you may,
He just happens to be on the same path as you."

Line 2214 - "Gummawn. Gummawn. Gummawn. Gummawn. Gummawn."

"It would seem like more than that to me, the same
As Hercules or Aeneas or some other true
Legend, giving what they have in the name

Of another, a hero. But different." "Indeed."
"In deed, and in intent. For who can divine
What goes on in his head? Though no deceit,

What does he know?" "He knows he's about to recline
With Tlön. The only one who could defeat
Him was himself, you just have to maintain the climb,

Then when you fall, you know how to get up again."
Fing, dispirited: "But not me. I must be
Carried." "You are not with Tlön yet. To begin,

You keep going, you keep moving, eventually
You obtain enough momentum to descend,
Like a stone in dense water settling in

To the dominion of time, the crusher of bones
To dust. Universal scale, infinitesimal zero.
You stand at the threshold and the wonder   2245

Is that you are not alone, even if you don't know.
It has all been done before. Why sorrow and groan?
The pressure is off. You just need to go on."

Jack broke out into the open at the same
Moment that a man approached from below.
They met at the top of the tower. Gazing

Line 2245 - "You stand at the threshold and the wonder
          Is that you're not alone."

Up at the last Texans drifting off along
The gulf stream winds. "Mooooooooooooo."
One cowboy sang a plaintive yodel song,

The sky a peach and yellow on cumulus,
The town of New Bedford was not sacred and wrong.
Fing had to be a diving homunculus.

"A game!" The man announced, without introduction
(Fing holding Douglass' hand with two hands):
"Politics! That is all there is to this production.

Forgive me if I do it no reverence;
It sickens my stomach to refluxion
To see scavenging, idolatrous dance

Over the corpus of the Presidency."
Douglass recognized the fierce and hapless man:
"If I recall, despite my hesitancy,

You are the impeached one." He: "That I am.
But nobody accepts credulously
That I committed high crimes. 'Twas a scam!

After Lincoln, the Union was divided.
'E pluribus unum' never was real.
All of those things we are taught to take pride in   2272

Are nothing but impossible ideals.
If I am a man, if I step over the line,
It is because that is how I feel

About how I and we need to progress.
Anybody can get hysterical
In reaction, but they are just playing chess."

Line 2272 - "All those things we are taught to take pride in
            Are nothing but impossible ideals."

"Your crime," nodded Douglass severely,
"Was simply an indiscretion. The reaction
Was over the top, political theater."

"Deep divisions revealed in that enactment,   2282
A cleaving at wounds which healed better
When we turned our attention against the Negro."

Another grizzled man appeared: "That fetter
Belongs to me as well. I have worn it five score
Years. But I will jump again together

With you Johnson." Johnson: "Hayes! We've done this before."
"This time we shall fall into Tlön, we deserve it.
What are the sins of a man once foresworn?

Line 2282 - "Deep divisions revealed in that enactment"

We renounced our wickedness, we observed
Such punishments as were proscribed. We bore
Malice toward none. Let us continue to preserve

Protect and defend. Let's move on from this
Limbo. Tlön will receive us. Let's go on."
Douglass took Fing aside: "These men miss

The point that they get heavier if they walk down."
Johnson and Hayes embraced each other, kissless.
They sidled to the ledge, having led none,

And leapt out over the street of the provincial
Town. They lowered slightly, as a bubble
Might if a wafting current providentially

Line 2313 - ...Jack leaned forward,
          And entered free fall.

Dipped through the expiring air. The double
Man felt their downward thrust and prodigiously
Shouted, "We are going down! No trouble!"

They clapped each other on the back and smiled.
Jack took Fing's hand from Douglass and said, "Gummawn."
Hauling Fing's arms over his shoulders, to dive

With Fing on his back. Fing begged Jack, "Will you hold on?"
Fing looked at Douglass: "If I could shit myself
I would." "Yes," Douglass replied, "fear is the last to go."

"Thank you." Douglass shook his head, and nodded:
"Good-bye," and he turned, and Jack leaned forward,   2313
And they entered free fall. Jack began singing:

"Michael rowed the boat ashore, alleluia!"
They went screaming by Hayes and Johnson, who were
Stalled well above the fast approaching ground,

Bobbing like they were caught in a draft,
Jack driving blissfully face first toward
The dusty street. Fing looked up. Night had come

In from the darkest blue-green of twilight.
He wondered if this would be the last thing he saw   2322
The screaming air, the approaching earth, and one star.

Line 2322 - ...the last thing he saw
          The screaming air, the approaching earth, and one star.